ZIBBY PAYNE

& THE PARTY PROBLEM

Zibby Payne & the Party Problem
Text © 2008 Alison Bell

Published by Lobster Press™
1620 Sherbrooke Street West, Suites C & D
Montréal, Québec   H3H 1C9
Tel. (514) 904-1100 • Fax (514) 904-1101 • www.lobsterpress.com

Publisher: Alison Fripp
Editors: Alison Fripp & Meghan Nolan
Editorial Assistants: Lindsay Cornish & Shiran Teitelbaum
Graphic Design & Production: Tammy Desnoyers

Library and Archives Canada Cataloguing in Publication

Bell, Alison
    Zibby Payne & the party problem / Alison Bell.

(Zibby Payne series)
ISBN 978-1-897073-69-8

    I. Title. II. Title: Zibby Payne and the party problem.
III. Series: Bell, Alison. Zibby Payne series.

PZ7.B41528Zip 2008   j813'.6   C2007-904820-X

Abercrombie & Fitch is a trademark of Abercrombie & Fitch Trading Co.; **Adidas** is a
trademark of adidas America, Inc.; **Barney** is a trademark of Lyons Partnership, L.P.;
Black Eyed Peas is a trademark of Black Eyed Peas; **Cinderella** is a trademark of Disney
Enterprises, Inc.; **Cookie Monster** is a trademark of Sesame Workshop Corporation;
Disney is a trademark of Disney Enterprises, Inc.; **Dumbo** is a trademark of Disney
Enterprises, Inc.; **Elmo** is a trademark of Sesame Workshop Corporation; **Elvis** is a
trademark of Elvis Presley Enterprises, Inc.; **Google** is a trademark of Google, Inc.;
Grover is a trademark of Sesame Workshop Corporation; **High School Musical** is the
trademark of Disney Enterprises, Inc.; **Hotel California** is the trademark of Warner Bros.
Publications U.S. Inc.; **iPod** is a trademark of Apple Inc.; **Life Savers** is a trademark of
Wrigley Jr. Company; **M&Ms** is a trademark of Mars, Incorporated Corporation; **Nestles
Crunch** is a trademark of Nestles Company, Inc.; **Polly Pocket** is a trademark of Origin
Products, Ltd.; **Shake 'N Bake** is a trademark of Kraft Foods, Inc.; **Simpsons** is a trademark
of Twentieth Century Fox Film Corporation; **Snow White and the Seven Dwarves** is a
trademark of Disney Enterprises, Inc.; **Sponge Bob** is a trademark of Viacom International
Inc.; **Sprite** is a trademark of The Coca-Cola Company; **Strawberry Shortcake** (the stickers)
is a trademark of Those Characters From Cleveland, Inc.; **Talbot** is a trademark of The
Classics Chicago, Inc.; **Target** is a trademark of Target Corporation; **The Beatles** is a
trademark of Apple Corps Limited; **The Eagles** is a trademark of Eagles, Ltd. and Eagles
Recording Co.; **Transformers** is a trademark of Hasbro, Inc.; **Twister** is a trademark of
Hasbro, Inc.; **Urban Outfitters** is a trademark of Urban Outfitters, Inc.

Printed and bound in the United States.

To editor extraordinaire, Meghan Nolan.

– Alison Bell

ZIBBY PAYNE

& THE PARTY PROBLEM

Written by

Alison Bell

Lobster Press™

CHAPTER 1

A BIRTHDAY INVITATION

"Don't put on those shoes," a voice next to Zibby Payne commanded.

Zibby, who had been sitting on a school bench changing into her Adidas cleats, stopped what she was doing and looked up. Her sometimes friend Amber was standing next to her with her hands on her hips.

"Why not?" Zibby asked. She was going to play soccer with the boys just as she did almost every lunchtime.

"I'm calling a super important meeting for all my peeps in five minutes at table twelve, and you need to be there," said Amber. "Everyone's coming, so you can forget soccer today."

Zibby rolled her eyes. She didn't want to meet with Amber & Friends – she wanted to play soccer. Back in the day – before sixth grade started – Amber used to be a nice, normal girl who played tetherball, wore jeans from Target, and did extra credit reports on whales. Now all she and her "peeps" cared about was Groovy Grapilicious lip gloss, stupid boy bands, and Urban Outfitters mini-skirts.

Zibby sat there, one cleat on, one cleat off, pondering what to do, when her best friend Sarah walked up and sat down next to her.

"What do you know about this meeting Amber's having?" asked Zibby. "Do I have to go? I mean, why should I?"

"Her birthday's next week, and she's handing out invitations to her party," said Sarah. "I heard her talking about it before school."

"Birthday invitations?" Zibby repeated to herself. This actually might be worth passing up soccer for, because despite Zibby's Less-Than-Fabulous feelings about Amber, Zibby had to admit that Amber always had really fun parties.

Zibby ripped off the cleat and put her green high-top back on. On the other foot, she wore one of Sarah's striped flats – she and Sarah wore one of each other's shoes almost every day as a sign of their friendship. Luckily, they'd always worn the same size shoe.

"I wonder what Amber's got planned this year," said Zibby.

"Remember back in second grade when she threw that Goldfish Gala?" said Sarah. "She gave each of us a goldfish in a little bowl."

"I named mine Stinky Cheese cuz he really stunk!" remembered Zibby. "But still, I loved that fish."

"Then last year we all went to that fancy restaurant where they cook the food at your table," said Sarah. "And the chef throws the veggies up in the air and does tricks with them."

"That place was awesome – even though just because

Ashton Kutcher owns it everyone thought he was going to personally greet us," said Zibby. "Like he doesn't have better things to do with his time!"

"That's for sure," said Sarah, nodding.

Suddenly Amber's voice boomed over to them from across the lunch yard. "Zibby, Sarah, get over here quick!" she yelled.

"The queen has summoned us," said Zibby, looking very serious. "We must obey her command."

"Be nice," Sarah said as she raised her eyebrows at Zibby.

"I will be, I swear," said Zibby.

They walked over to Amber, who was sitting on top of the table, and stood at the back of a crowd of girls surrounding her.

"Now that you're all here, I have a surprise I want to share with you," said Amber. She pulled a pile of bright pink envelopes out of an Abercrombie & Fitch shopping bag. On each envelope, a girl's name was written in silver cursive handwriting.

"Cool invites," said Camille, Amber's best friend – or as Zibby called her, "Amber's clone."

"Pink – what a shocker," Zibby said to herself as she looked at the invitation. That was another thing that bugged Zibby – Amber's devotion to wimpy pastel colors like pink. Zibby preferred a strong red or blue any day.

"Here's yours," Amber said as she handed an invitation to Camille. "And yours" – she gave one to Zibby – "and yours, too," she held a pink envelope out to

Sarah. One by one, she passed out all of the invitations.

"But wait!" Amber ordered. "Don't open them until I tell you."

"Woops," said Zibby, who had already ripped a corner of her envelope off. She quickly covered the torn piece with her fingers and tried to be more patient.

"Okay," Amber said as she sat up straighter. "At the count of three, you can all open them. One, two, three ... now!"

The girls eagerly tore open their envelopes and pulled out their invitations. But before anyone even got a chance to read the invitation, a girl named Savannah cried out, "There's something in my envelope – silver glitter and a special coupon!" She reached into the envelope, grabbed a pinch of glitter, and threw it into the air.

"Mine, too!" squealed Camille.

"Same here!" came another voice behind Zibby.

Zibby was confused. There wasn't any glitter or coupon in *her* envelope. She even turned it over and shook it hard to make sure. But no matter how hard she shook it, nothing fell out. Absolutely nothing at all.

CHAPTER 2

COUPON CONFUSION

"I didn't get any glitter or a coupon," Zibby was about to say when she looked around and saw she wasn't alone. Sarah's envelope didn't contain anything more than the invitation. Neither did about half of the other girls' envelopes.

What does this mean? Zibby wondered. The other girls began to read their invitations, so Zibby did too, hoping it might answer her question.

The invitation, which, like the envelope, was pink with silver writing, read:

You're invited ...
To the birthday party of the ~~year~~ ~~decade~~ ~~century~~ millennium!
This Friday, from 6 - 9 pm
At Amber's place
Text your RSVP to Amber's cell: 555-9110
Be there or be a total loser!
And congratulations if your envelope contained silver glitter and a coupon. This means you're entitled to a special party prize! Don't forget to bring the coupon with you to the party.

A special party prize? Zibby thought. Zibby peered into her envelope one more time, as if she was waiting for a coupon to magically sprout. But it was still emptier than

11

empty. Camille, who was standing in front of Zibby, was admiring her coupon, so Zibby stood on her tippy toes behind her to get a closer look. Sarah, standing next to her, did the same. In cursive silver handwriting was written, *"Special Party Prize for Special Friends. Non-transferable."*

Zibby frowned and whispered to Sarah, "I don't get it. What's up with these coupons and this 'special friend' stuff?"

But Sarah didn't answer. She shrugged, then she broke free from the crowd and began to quickly walk away.

Zibby hurried after her. "So how come we didn't get one?" she asked. "And where was our glitter?"

"I guess we're not 'special' enough," said Sarah.

"Maybe she left them out by mistake," said Zibby.

"I don't think so," said Sarah. "Amber doesn't make mistakes like that."

"So she isn't giving us – or some of the other girls – coupons *on purpose*?" asked Zibby.

"I guess so," mumbled Sarah.

"Only some girls get a special prize and are considered special?" Zibby continued, slowly catching on.

"Yeah, I think that's what she's doing," Sarah repeated in a low voice.

"That's stupid! And unfair!" yelled Zibby. "And bad party manners, too!"

"I can't believe she'd leave me out," Sarah said. "Or you, either. We've known her since kindergarten." She hung her head down and looked as if she might cry.

"Oh, don't feel bad! Who cares, anyway?" Zibby

said. "Besides, I just remembered – my parents are out Friday night, so I think I'm sleeping over at your place, if that's okay with you. And *that* will be fun!"

"A sleepover sounds good, but still, those coupons ..." Sarah's voice trailed off just as the bell rang, signaling class was about to begin.

"Don't think about them anymore," said Zibby, trying to cheer Sarah up as they hurried to their classroom. "Let's just get to class and forget all about Amber's stupid party."

Sarah gave Zibby a half-hearted smile as the two separated at the door and walked to their desks. Zibby was just pulling out her English folder from her backpack when Camille and Amber rushed by.

"This is going to be the most amazing party ever," Camille said as she dashed through the rows of desks, practically hitting Zibby in the face with her coupon.

"I know!" Amber giggled.

So much for forgetting, Zibby thought crankily, slamming her English folder down on her desk.

"Hey, Sarah," Zibby whispered loudly across the room. When Sarah turned to look, Zibby mouthed the word "coupon" then stuck a finger in her mouth as if she were gagging herself. Sarah smiled.

Zibby, now feeling satisfied, leaned back in her chair. But as she watched Camille in the row in front of her carefully smooth her coupon out with the palm of her hand, then reverently place it in her English grammar workbook, Zibby was hit with a funny feeling. A feeling she had when she first started playing soccer at recess and none of the boys chose her for their teams. A feeling that she had to admit didn't feel very good.

CHAPTER 3

THE EXPLAIN GAME

The next day at lunch, all anyone could talk about was The Coupons. Amber had run to the office to pick up a strawberry smoothie and pesto chicken sandwich her mom had dropped off as part of her pre-birthday week of hand-delivered lunches, and in the Party Hostess's absence, the girls let loose about how they really felt.

"They're so snotty," said a girl named Lyla who was upset because she lived next door to Amber and hadn't gotten a coupon.

"I think they're mean," said Sarah, nodding.

"Mega-mean," sniffed another non-coupon holder, Grace.

"I'm just happy I got one!" admitted one FOA – Friend of Amber's – named Kelsey.

"Me, too!" said Savannah.

"She wouldn't tell me what the special prize is, but I just know it's gonna be really sweet!" cried out Camille, clapping her hands together excitedly.

Lyla shot Camille a "how rude" look, but Camille didn't seem to notice.

Zibby did, however. She'd been sitting there uncharacteristically quiet during the entire conversation, trying to eat her salmon and pickle sandwich quickly in order to get out on the field and play soccer with the boys. But suddenly she felt she might throw up if she had to listen to one more word of Coupon Chatter! "These coupons stink, and I'm going to do something about them," she declared, swallowing the last bite of her sandwich and tossing her baggy into a nearby trash can.

"What are you going to do?" asked Lyla.

"Boycott the party," said Zibby. The idea just came to her like that, but it felt as if it was the right thing to do.

"No!" the other girls gasped.

"But everyone's going to be there!" said Grace.

"And Amber's parties are always awesome!" said Kelsey.

"I get the feeling this one won't be," said Zibby.

"Um, Zibby," said Sarah. "Don't forget, you're spending the night at my house that night, so unless you want to hang out with my parents alone, you sort of have to go."

"Oh," Zibby frowned. But then she smiled as she was hit with another Very Good Idea.

"Okay, then if I have to go, I'm going to have a little chat with Amber."

"About what?" asked Sarah.

"I'm going to tell her she should forget those stupid coupons," Zibby said.

"But I like mine!" protested Savannah.

"Me, too." Kelsey stomped her foot.

"She'll never listen to you anyway, Zibby," said Sarah.

"Maybe not, but I've got to try," said Zibby. Without waiting to hear what anyone else had to say, she stood up from the table and strode off to the office to find Amber.

But just as she reached the office door, she felt a little pang of guilt and stopped. Earlier in the year, she'd started an Exclusive Tomboy Club, and she hadn't included any of her friends, not even Sarah. So it wasn't as if Zibby had always been fair about including people herself. What right did she have to confront Amber?

On the other hand, the only reason why Zibby started the club was because she felt as if her friends didn't like her anymore. So the situation was totally different. Plus, her club had been a flop. A big one. And if someone had told her not to create the club in the first place, that person would have been doing her a favor. Just as, if you thought about it, she was actually doing Amber a favor now by letting her know her coupons were a big flop!

Zibby pulled open the office door and almost ran smack into the Party Princess herself.

"Hey!" Zibby greeted her. "I need to talk to you!"

"About what?" asked Amber, letting Zibby hold the door open for her since her hands were full with the special lunch delivery.

"Your party," said Zibby.

"I'm starving," Amber said, looking annoyed. "Can it wait?"

"No," said Zibby firmly.

"Okay, then," sighed Amber. "What is it?" she asked as she sucked on her smoothie. When she took her lips off the straw to swallow, Zibby noticed that the tip of the straw was Groovy Grapilicious purple.

"I wanted to let you know that you shouldn't have coupons at your party because the girls who didn't get them are really upset," said Zibby.

"Really?" asked Amber, looking surprised. "They shouldn't be. I just have some really cool stuff to hand out, but I don't have enough for everyone, so I thought of the coupon idea. Oh, and the only reason you didn't get one was because I know you wouldn't like the special prize. But, for sure, you are still totally special to me, Zibby." She gave Zibby a big smile and took another slurp of her smoothie.

"This isn't about me," exclaimed Zibby. "It's about the other girls, like Sarah. I don't care about getting a coupon or being your special friend, but they do."

"Oh. Well, explain it to them, will ya, Zibby?" said Amber. "Tell Sarah and everyone that they're all special friends in my heart, even if they didn't get a coupon. Luv you all! Time to chow now," she waved her drink at Zibby and then hurried away, passing Sarah.

"So what did she say?" asked Sarah as she caught up to Zibby.

"Something about how we're all *special friends* in her heart even if we didn't get a coupon," said Zibby. "I didn't really have a clue about what she was talking about, but I'm pretty sure she's not going to change her mind about the coupons."

"I didn't think she would," said Sarah.

Zibby was still replaying the conversation in her mind when Lyla rushed up to her. And Grace. And everyone else who hadn't gotten a coupon.

"Hey, Zibby," yelled Lyla. "Amber told us to talk to you!"

"She did?" asked Zibby, confused.

"Yeah, she's over at the lunch tables, and she said you'd fill us all in on the party and why only some people got coupons," said Grace.

"Tell us *everything*," demanded a girl named Katherine. "Don't leave out one little detail."

"Come on, we're waiting!" urged Lyla.

Zibby opened her mouth, then closed it, speechless. *I can't believe this!* she thought. *I don't even want to go to this stupid party and now I have to explain it to everyone!*

CHAPTER 4

A WIMPY WALKOUT

Like it or not, Zibby was stuck rehashing Amber's Theory of Coupons not once, but several times that week. And after about the fourth time explaining that they were all "special friends in Amber's heart," the girls finally seemed satisfied with the answer.

Besides, they had a new, more pressing worry to wrestle with: what *not* to wear. Two days before the party, Amber ordered them to wear fancy dresses to the party – but not black, because that was reserved just for the Birthday Girl's attire. And white was off-limits to everyone but Camille, the "BFF" to the birthday girl. So everyone else had to hustle to find a dress in an Amber-sanctioned color.

Zibby, however, didn't sweat about the dress code one bit. She didn't even own a dress – unless you counted the frilly one at the back of her closet that she was forced to wear when her Grandma Betty took her to a fancy restaurant called The Oaks. She had planned on wearing her usual jeans and T-shirt to the party. She did make one concession, however. She traded in her scuffed up green high-tops for her brand-new, spotless red ones.

On the night of the party, Sarah's mom dropped

Zibby and Sarah off at Amber's house, a large Colonial with a brick facade. Camille was sitting at the front door, holding a clipboard with a piece of paper and a pen attached to it.

"Hi, Camille," said Zibby, reaching for the door handle.

"I see you didn't get the 'dresses only' message," Camille said snottily.

"I got it. I just didn't follow it," said Zibby.

Camille gave a little snort of disapproval, then said, "And, before you step through that door, I need your names."

Sarah and Zibby exchanged a glance.

"It's *us*," said Zibby. "You know our names."

"Names, please," Camille repeated, a little snappily.

"We've known you since we were making pretzel reindeer together in kindergarten. If you've forgotten our names, I'm really worried about you," said Zibby.

"Just say your name, Zibby!" hissed Camille. "I've got a list here of everyone who was invited to the party, and I promised Amber I'd ask everyone for their names, then check them off on this sheet. That's what they do at those really exclusive clubs the celebs go to. If you're not on the list, you're not allowed in."

"But we *are* on the list," protested Zibby. "Plus, *you* just *said* my name for me."

"It doesn't matter," snapped Camille. "*You* have to say it!"

Zibby rolled her eyes. If Camille wanted names, okay, she'd give her names.

"Mia Hamm and Brandi Chastain," Zibby said, just as Sarah was saying, "Sarah Schroeder and Zibby Payne."

"Thank *you*, Sarah," Camille said, glaring at Zibby. "You two may go in. Party's in the living room."

"Thank you," said Zibby. "We're so relieved we made the cut!"

The girls walked into the entry hall and were immediately struck by how loud and dark it was. The lights were turned off, so they could hardly see a thing. Hip-hop music with the bass turned up high vibrated off the walls.

"This way!" Amber was suddenly at their side, pushing them toward the living room. Well, Zibby couldn't really make out the girl's features, but it sounded like Amber. And smelled grapey like Amber.

"It's pretty dark," said Zibby as they entered the room. The living room was just as dark as the entry hall except for a few candles lit over the fireplace.

"I know, isn't it great?" gushed Amber. "This is how they light all the clubs the celebrities go to so they won't be discovered by any paparazzi. Plus, it's a lot more fun and mysterious this way!"

"Real fun and mysterious," said Zibby gloomily after knocking into a chair. She carefully made her way over to the food table, where she poured herself a Sprite in a paper cup covered with glitter, and ate a few chips.

"Just like I predicted, this party is terrible," said Zibby. "Where's the Goldfish Gala when you need it?"

"Or the performing chef?" asked Sarah with a sigh.

"Wake me up if something interesting happens," said Zibby, closing her eyes and giving a fake snore.

Just then, the music stopped in the middle of a Black Eyed Peas song and the lights flipped on.

As Zibby blinked to adjust her eyes to the brightness, Amber stepped up to the front of the room and positioned herself next to a table where an iPod and speakers were set up. A large cardboard box sat on the floor next to the table.

"I'd like to thank you for coming to my birthday bash," said Amber, smiling. "I hope you're all having an awesome time just like me."

In your glitter-covered dreams, thought Zibby.

"And now, here comes the special part of the evening that I know many of you have been looking forward to all night," she continued. "Can I please have all the girls with coupons join me up here?"

Camille, Savannah, Kelsey, and the rest of Amber's special "peeps" rushed up to stand next to Amber. The girls left behind suddenly got very interested in studying their feet, as if the toes of their sandals and ballet slippers were the most fascinating things they'd ever seen. But not Zibby. She fixed Amber with a Big Stare to let her know she was coupon-less and proud.

"Coupons, please," said Amber, turning to the girls next to her and sticking out her hand. "You did bring them with you, didn't you?" she asked.

The Chosen Few eagerly smashed their coupons into Amber's palm. Amber examined each one and then placed them in a pile on the table. "Thank you," she said, and then turned her attention back to the coupon holders. "You've probably been wondering what these coupons are for. And now, finally, you're going to find out!"

She bent down and put her hand on the box on the floor. "What I have right here are seven new BB5 T-shirts with a photo of their latest CD cover on them – straight from their recording label because my dad knows the designer who made the shirts. So put them on!" She reached into the box, drew out a handful of T-shirts, and threw them at the girls. They squealed with joy as they reached out to catch the shirts, then quickly pulled them on over their dresses.

"And now," Amber continued, "I'd like you few to join me in a little dance to BB5's hit new song that is currently the number one downloaded song – 'I May Be a Brat, But I Know You Like That.'" Amber reached for the switch above the table and dimmed the lights, and the select group of girls began to dance.

Zibby couldn't believe it! She personally hated BB5. It was a weak bubblegum boy band that couldn't begin to compete with the classic rock and roll bands she listened to, such as The Eagles and The Beatles. So Amber's explanation that she hadn't given Zibby a coupon because she knew Zibby wouldn't like the prize made sense.

But Sarah loved BB5. So did Grace. And Lyla. And probably all the other girls too. That wasn't fair. Plus, to quote one of her mom's Favorite Expressions, *if you don't have enough for everyone, you shouldn't give out any at all!*

"Now everyone else get on up here and shake your booties!" yelled Amber.

But none of the other girls made a move to dance. Lyla sat down on a chair while Grace poured herself another cup of orange soda. And Sarah just stood there as if someone had hot-glued her shoes to the floor.

This is ridiculous, Zibby thought. *I've had enough!* She turned to Sarah, Lyla, and the rest of the excluded girls. "This party is undemocratic, and I am personally protesting it by walking out right now," Zibby announced. "Who is with me?"

Without waiting for an answer, Zibby began to slowly walk out of the room. "Okay, follow me," she called out behind her. "And let's make an anti-Amber demonstration together."

As she marched through the entry hall, she burst out in a chant, "There's no chance I'm gonna dance." She kept repeating it over and over, louder and louder, as she swung open the front door and strutted outside.

"THERE'S NO CHANCE I'M GONNA DANCE!" she yelled out one more time, then whirled around in triumph.

"That was great, wasn't it?" she yelled. "We really showed her ... "

Her voice trailed off, and her smile disappeared as if it had been zapped by a laser gun. Not one girl – not even Sarah – had followed her.

CHAPTER 5

HISTORY REPEATS ITSELF

"I can't believe you didn't come outside with me!" Zibby yelled into her kitchen phone.

It was late afternoon the next day, and she and Sarah were rehashing Amber's party... again. They'd already discussed Zibby's Lonely Protest of One several times, but Zibby couldn't drop it.

"I know, I know," pleaded Sarah. "But like I said, the party was so weird, I didn't want to make it even weirder."

Zibby was silent. "Weird" sure did describe the party. Especially after Zibby had to slink back into Amber's house and listen to BB5 songs for another hour – with Amber shooting her Death Stares the entire time – before Sarah's mom came to pick them up.

"You know what?" Zibby said finally. "It's all right. I'm just glad that stupid party is over and we don't ever have to think about it again."

"Thanks, Zibby," said Sarah. "Anyway, I've got to run because – "

"Hey, I just got something in the mail," Zibby interrupted as she checked out an envelope her mom had handed to her. "And it looks like another invitation. I don't know if I should open it, though, if the party's gonna be like Amber's."

"Oh, come on. Who's it from?" Sarah asked.

Zibby tore open the invitation. "From Savannah," she said. She quickly scanned the invitation, which read:

Savannah's turning 12!

Please join me next Friday at the Good Times Roller Skating Rink at 7:00 pm. Have your parents drive you to the rink, then we'll drive you back to my house for a sleepover.

RSVP to Savannah: 555-9087

"And good news," Zibby said. "It's gonna be a roller skating party. No special coupons or prizes this time."

"I hope I'm invited," Sarah said, her voice sounding small.

"Of course you are," said Zibby. They'd both known Savannah forever. Maybe Zibby knew her a bit better, but not much.

"Hey, wait," Sarah yelled. Zibby heard footsteps and something rustling. "I just ran out to the mailbox and I have one too."

"See?" said Zibby.

"Oh gosh," said Sarah. "I've really got to run. I'm almost late. Talk to you later about Savannah's party!" And she hung up.

"I wonder where she had to go?" Zibby asked herself. But within seconds, she'd forgotten she even asked the question. Because all she could think about was how much fun Savannah's party was going to be.

* * *

"Slow down, crazy roller girl!" Sarah yelled, coming up behind Zibby, who was on her bazillionth lap around the roller skating rink the night of Savannah's party.

"Catch me if you can!" Zibby said, speeding up.

"I am *so* going to get you!" yelled Sarah. She put her head down and skated as hard as she could. She finally reached Zibby, and the two sprinted around the rink together one more time.

"I need a break," gasped Sarah.

"Me, too," panted Zibby.

They skated over to the handrail where Camille, Savannah, and Kelsey were standing.

"Great party!" Zibby said to Savannah, her cheeks glowing.

"Thanks," said Savannah. "And if you're hungry, the Skate Shack over there is open. You get can anything you want."

Zibby and Sarah looked at each other. "We're there!" they said in unison. The two girls pulled off their skates and walked over in their socks to order up two burgers and Sprites.

By the time the end of the party rolled around at 9:00 pm, Zibby was tired, but not too tired to stay up all night – which is exactly what she planned to do at Savannah's sleepover. She was working on her own personal record of Sleepless Sleepovers. So far, she was four for four, and after this party, if she could stay awake, she'd be five for five.

Zibby returned her skates with Sarah and was about to find Savannah's mom to get a ride, when Sarah's mom walked through the door.

"Hey, what's your mom doing here?" Zibby asked Sarah. "Savannah's parents are taking us home."

"No they aren't," said Sarah. "The invitation said our parents are supposed to pick us up."

"No," insisted Zibby. "It said that Savannah's parents are giving us a ride to the sleepover."

Sarah blinked. "What sleepover?" she asked.

Oh no, Zibby thought. To Sarah, she said, "Just a sec – let me check something." She scanned the room and found Savannah standing by the front door next to Amber.

"Hey, Savannah," Zibby said as she ran up to her and pulled her aside. "There's been a mix-up. Sarah doesn't know about the sleepover."

"Oh." Savannah frowned. Then she whispered, "Not everyone was invited. My mom said I can only have six girls sleep over, and I invited 12 to go roller skating. So only some girls got the sleepover part of the invitation."

"You mean, Sarah isn't invited to sleep over?" asked Zibby.

"Right."

"But I just told her it was a sleepover!" exclaimed Zibby.

"I told everyone to keep it a *secret* – that was on the invitation," said Savannah.

"It wasn't on mine!" said Zibby defensively.

"Maybe I forgot to write it on yours," said Savannah, waving her hand as if to say she was tired of the topic. "Look, you caused this problem, so just think of something to tell her. I don't have time to worry about it. I need to gather the rest of the girls who are sleeping over." She headed back over toward Amber.

Zibby stood there, miserable. What was she going to tell Sarah? And what was she going to do? She made a quick decision. "Wait a minute," she called over to Savannah, catching up to her before she could reach Amber. "I appreciate you inviting me to the sleepover, but I wouldn't feel right going without Sarah. So I'm going to get a ride home with Sarah's mom instead."

Savannah's mouth fell open. Then she snarled, "Zibby Payne, I wasted one of my sleepover invites on you when I could have invited someone else! You can really be a big *pain* sometimes, you know that?"

"Well, I'm sorry," Zibby shot back, totally annoyed now. "If you'd invited everyone in the first place, you wouldn't be having this problem!" Zibby whirled around and walked back over to Sarah, who was now slumping against the wall with her arms crossed.

"It was all just a mix-up," she said to Sarah. "I got confused. I'm catching a ride home with you, if that's okay."

"You don't have to protect me," said Sarah. "I figured it out while you were talking to Savannah. Grace and Lyla weren't invited to the sleepover either. Or some of the other girls."

"I'm so sorry," said Zibby. "I'm sure she wanted you, it's just that her mom said she could only have a few girls sleep over."

"It's not that I really care about the sleepover – I'm tired anyway. It's just that I feel sort of stupid," said Sarah softly.

"But you're not – they're the stupid ones!" yelled Zibby, thinking about not only Savannah but Amber, as the two girls followed Sarah's mom out to the car. "What are they thinking with all these snotty parties? It makes me, it makes me ... I know," she suddenly smiled as she was hit with one of her Very Good Ideas. One that would cheer up Sarah and the rest of the girls who were left out and would erase the memory of Amber and Savannah's parties.

"What?" asked Sarah as the two girls hopped into the backseat, slammed the doors shut, and strapped on their seat belts.

"I'm going to have a party!" Zibby declared. "A party where everyone is invited and everyone is treated the same. A great party – no, the best party ever! And I'll have it in two weeks – on the 18th!"

"Really?" said Sarah, perking up. "Do you think your parents will let you?"

"Of course they will! They taught me to stand up for my rights and the rights of others. And Savannah and Amber are suppressing our right to fair and equal parties."

"That's right!" said Sarah, nodding her head vigorously.

"A party for all, and all for the party!" exclaimed Zibby.

"And I'll help," said Sarah.

During the rest of the drive home, the two girls made up a guest list on an old grocery store receipt they found on the floor. When they were done, they'd written down twenty-four names.

"That's everyone we're friends with, sometimes friends with, used-to-be friends with, and want-to-be friends with," said Zibby. "We haven't left out anyone!"

"Your party will more than make up for tonight," said Sarah. "I'm so happy!"

Me, too," said Zibby, settling down in her seat satisfactorily. But then one small little worry popped up in her brain. Twenty-four guests did sound like a lot. Her parents *would* go for this plan – wouldn't they?

CHAPTER 6

THE MOST INCLUSIVE PARTY ON THE PLANET

"Score!" Zibby yelled into the phone when she called Sarah the next day. "My parents said yes! At first, they said no because there are so many kids and it's not even my birthday and it's gonna cost money and how am I going to pay for it all? But then I explained all about Amber and Savannah's parties and how I wanted a party that included everyone, and they went for it! Turns out that my mom didn't get invited to some big graduation party back when she was in sixth grade, so she says it's good 'karmic payback' – whatever that means. Anyway, I get to do it!"

"Sweet," said Sarah. "Want me to start making phone calls and tell everyone to save the date? Then you can send out invitations later."

"Sounds good to me," said Zibby, smiling. *Everything* was sounding good to her right now.

* * *

The next day at school, the first two people Zibby ran into on the blacktop were Amber and Camille.

"We talked to Sarah, and we're both coming to your

party," said Amber, flashing a big grapey smile.

Ever since Zibby's protest at Amber's party, Amber had been pretty much ignoring her. But Amber never wanted to miss out on anything, and Zibby guessed that now that *she* was having a party, Amber was willing to be her friend again.

"My mom said I can get new shoes for your party," said Camille.

"*My* mom said I can get new shoes *and* a new dress!" gushed Amber.

"The party's casual," said Zibby. "So you don't have to wear a dress. Wear jeans if you want."

"I'm wearing jeans," said Sarah, smiling at Zibby.

"I always wear dresses to parties," Amber said a bit sharply. "And I always get a new one."

"Yeah, don't tell Amber's mom it's casual, or she won't buy her one," said Camille.

Maybe that also accounts for Amber's new, improved attitude toward me, thought Zibby. *She wants some new clothes and right now I'm her ticket to another Abercrombie & Fitch shopping spree.*

"Wear whatever you want," said Zibby, remembering the inclusive spirit of her party. "There are no rules at my party."

Amber pulled out a tube of lip gloss from the outside pocket of her backpack and applied a fresh coat. "So," she said, as she put the gloss back into the pocket. "Who else is coming to your party?"

"Everyone!" said Zibby happily.

"What do you mean, *everyone*?" asked Amber, narrowing her eyes. "Let me see the guest list."

"I don't have it with me," said Zibby. Actually the crumpled receipt was in her pocket, but why should she show it to Amber? She didn't need Amber's approval of who she'd invited.

Amber looked at Camille and said, "I'll bet she's not inviting 'everyone,' like she says she is."

"I am too!" said Zibby hotly, just as Sarah protested, "Yes, she is!"

Zibby fished around in her pocket, and pulled out the list.

"There," Zibby handed it to Amber. "You can see for yourself."

"Nice notepaper," Amber said sarcastically, pinching the receipt between her two fingers as if it were a dead rat. She then quickly studied the list.

"Hmm," she sniffed. Then she admitted, "That *is* a lot of names."

"Told you," said Zibby, plucking the paper out of Amber's hand and cramming it back into her pocket.

Just then, Grace came running up to Zibby and threw her arms around her. "Thanks for having a non-special-coupon, non-secret-sleepover party," she whispered loudly so everyone could hear. "Your party's gonna be the best."

"I know," Zibby said. Grace skipped off to join Lyla and some other girls standing nearby, and as she did, Lyla gave Zibby a big thumbs up.

Amber, who had overheard Grace's not-so-quiet

comment, shot Zibby one of her Death Stares. "If you're still upset about the coupons, I really can't help it," she said with a toss of her hair. "I think I explained myself quite clearly before, and it's time you all got over it."

"I *am* over it," said Zibby. "My party's just going to be different, that's all."

Amber opened her mouth and looked as if she was about to say something when suddenly, she pointed her finger to the right of her. "Loser alert – times two," she whispered to Camille. "Hold your breath – it might be contagious!" She pinched her nose shut. Camille giggled and held her nose, too.

Zibby turned her head to see who they were talking about and saw that Vanessa Heartgabel and Franny Dewberry were walking by. Zibby hated to hear anyone be called a loser, but she had to admit, she didn't exactly have Warm 'n Fuzzy Feelings toward Vanessa and Franny. Vanessa was not only the weirdest girl in sixth grade – she carried a Barney lunch box and wore her hair in three pigtails – but she was the one responsible for ruining Zibby's tomboy club. While Vanessa *seemed* tough and strong, it turned out she was the absolute worst tomboy ever and couldn't even play a few minutes worth of soccer without falling down and getting hurt.

And Franny had been mad at Zibby ever since the sixth grade play because she blamed Zibby for not getting a speaking part in the production. Even though it really wasn't Zibby's fault, Franny acted as if it was. Zibby had been ducking her ever since, especially since Franny's new "BFF" was Vanessa.

"Hi," huffed Vanessa as she passed by the girls. Franny just put her head down and didn't say anything.

"Like I said, what losers!" said Amber, unpinching her nose and taking a deep breath once Vanessa and Franny were a few yards away.

"Don't say that again," said Zibby

"Oh get real, Zibby," said Amber. "You think they're losers too. I didn't see them on your guest list, did I?"

"I can't invite the whole school, can I?" Zibby protested.

Amber and Camille exchanged an "I told you so" look, while Sarah sympathetically put a hand on Zibby's arm and gave her a reassuring pat. But despite Sarah's reassurance, Zibby's stomach gave a little lurch. Because as hard as she was trying, maybe her party wasn't as much for "everybody" as she thought it was.

CHAPTER 7

THE INCREDIBLE GROWING GUEST LIST

Later that day while walking with Sarah to lunch, Zibby saw Franny and Vanessa sitting all alone together at a table. "Do you think I should invite them?" Zibby asked Sarah, thinking that the two of them looked Pathetic & Lonely. "I feel bad for them, being called losers."

Sarah thought for a moment. "They'd probably be pretty happy if you did, because I bet they don't get that many invitations," she said. "And it *is* in the spirit of your party, even if they aren't really our friends. Besides, they're not really that bad. Actually, if you want to know, Vanessa and I – "

"What do you think my parents would say about adding more guests?" interrupted Zibby.

"Two's not that many," said Sarah

"That's true," said Zibby. "Plus, it might be funny to see the look on Amber's face when she sees who she calls the two 'losers' at my party. Okay, I'll do it."

She marched over to Franny and Vanessa's table. Vanessa was polishing her Barney lunchbox with a wadded up napkin. Franny was pulling the crusts off a soggy sandwich.

"Hey there," said Zibby. "Didn't mean to interrupt anything."

"Just shining up the Barnster," said Vanessa.

Franny put down her sandwich and looked up at Zibby expectantly.

"Um," Zibby cleared her throat. "I just wanted to let you know that I'm throwing a party at my house. Invitations will be coming, and you're definitely getting one."

"Getting *what*?" asked Franny suspiciously, as if she hadn't heard what Zibby had said.

"An invitation ... to my party," said Zibby.

"Oh," Franny said as she started to smile.

Vanessa put down her lunch box. "Thanks, Zibby," she said as she smiled widely, flashing a blob of something brown between her teeth that seemed to live there permanently. "That's my first party invitation I've gotten for like ... forever!"

"We'd love to come," said Franny. "Oh, and this means I'm not mad at you anymore about the play. I forgive you and will ask my parents, grandparents, aunts, uncles, and cousins to finally forget how you took away the only speaking part I'll probably ever get in my life. And my great-aunt Olivia, too. And Kendell, my great-aunt's nephew once removed who lives out of state."

"Um, thanks," said Zibby. "You sure you didn't leave out anybody in your family?"

Franny thought for a moment. "No – that's everyone whose been hating your guts," she said cheerily.

"Okay, then," said Zibby, not knowing how to respond. "Catch you later."

"Okeedokey," said Vanessa. That was another odd thing about Vanessa – she said "okeedokey" a lot.

"Thanks, Zibby," Franny said again.

As Zibby walked back to Sarah, she glanced over her shoulder at the two girls, and they were smiling and hugging each other.

"See," said Sarah, who'd watched the entire exchange. "You did the right thing."

"I guess so," said Zibby, who wasn't so sure. At least Franny's family didn't detest her anymore, but she sure hoped that sometime before her party, Vanessa would discover the joys of dental floss!

* * *

Walking home from school that day, Zibby's soccer buddy Matthew caught up with her. Well, actually he was more than that. He'd also been the co-star in the play with Zibby. A play where they had to kiss. A play that almost wrecked Zibby's entire life and her friendship with Matthew. But now that the kiss was over, it was O-V-E-R. Matthew and Zibby both acted as if it had never happened, which was just the way Zibby wanted it.

"Hey, tomboy," he said. "Long time no see."

It was true. Due to all of the drama surrounding the parties that Amber and Savannah had thrown, Zibby had been spending more time with the girls and less time out on the soccer field. And now that she had her own party to plan, she'd be spending even *less* time playing soccer.

"I know," she said. "I've been busy."

"Yeah, I heard all about your big party," said

Matthew. "For *all* of your friends."

"Yep," said Zibby. "Everyone's coming!"

"Really?" asked Matthew. "I just can't help but feel as if you're leaving out a few people."

"No way," exclaimed Zibby. "I even invited Franny and Vanessa. You can't get more 'everyone' than that."

"Really?" said Matthew. "It seems to me that you're leaving out some pretty important people in your life."

"Like who?" Zibby demanded, stopping and turning to face him.

"Like me," he replied.

"But you don't count," said Zibby. "You're a boy, and only girls are coming."

"I don't count? Ouch!" Matthew hit his chest as if she'd punched him.

"You know what I mean," said Zibby. "The party's just for girls."

"Why can't you invite boys?" Matthew asked.

"It's just that ... no one does it. Girls just have girls over."

"Maybe it's time for a change then." Matthew looked at her eagerly.

Boys – at her party? When she already had invited twenty-four – make that twenty-six – girls?

"I just don't think it would work," Zibby said.

Matthew hung his head. "It's okay," he said, glancing up at her with a hurt look. "I'll do something else the day of your party. Like sit around and watch Simpsons re-runs or something else, all by myself, all alone." He turned around and started walking back to school. "All alone, that's what I'll be," he called back to her.

Zibby knew Matthew was trying to make her feel guilty. And she knew she really shouldn't invite any more guests. But on the other hand, she'd just invited Franny and Vanessa, kids she didn't even like. And was it really fair to exclude Matthew, her good friend, just because he was a boy? Before she knew what she was doing, she whirled around and yelled out, "Okay, you can come. You and Zane and Drew and the rest of the soccer gang. You're all invited!"

"Really?" Matthew turned around and gave her a big smile. "You sure, tomboy?"

"I'm sure," she yelled out.

Matthew gave her two thumbs up then continued on his way.

And, for a second, Zibby was really sure.

But the next second, she wanted to kick herself.

Counting Matthew and the rest of the boys she played soccer with made eight more guests. If you also added Vanessa and Franny, that upped the number of extra guests to 10. That meant that the party had grown from 24 kids to 34. Her parents were going to kill her for inviting so many people.

And what were the girls going to think? They'd probably hate the idea of a co-ed party! Some of the girls were so shy around boys they could hardly even say "hi" when near them. She could just see it now – boys on one side of the room, girls on the other – her entire party One Long Uncomfortable Silence!

What had she done?

CHAPTER 8

MISS PARTY POPULAR

That entire evening, Zibby couldn't relax, worrying that she'd made the Worst Party Decision in the History of Entertaining. She didn't tell her parents that she'd invited more guests because she was afraid of how they'd react. And she was dreading facing all the girls at school the next morning and listening to their complaints that she, Zibby Payne, had broke the unwritten law of parties by inviting boys.

But the next morning at school, something strange happened. Something good-strange.

"Way to go, Zibby!" Savannah ran up to her on the blacktop and threw her arms around her. "I heard all about the boys coming and I can't wait! I wish I'd thrown a boy-girl party!"

"You totally rock," squealed Kelsey, who was trailing behind Savannah with several other girls.

"My mom said that ordinarily, I wouldn't be able to go to a coed party, but since you're throwing it, and my parents trust yours so much, I can," said Lyla.

"This makes up for you inviting those losers," said Amber, tossing her hair.

Zibby knew she meant Franny and Vanessa – *that*

news must have also gotten around.

The group of girls continued to chat about Zibby's party until the warning bell rang.

"Can you believe it?" Zibby asked Sarah as they walked to class. "I was worried they'd all hate the idea. They love it!"

"And inviting the boys fits right into the idea of including everyone, too," said Sarah.

"I know," said Zibby, happily. "And to think that I almost told Matthew he couldn't come!"

Zibby's party continued to be the Big Topic at both recesses and lunch that day. It wasn't just the sixth graders who were talking about her party, either. Even the fifth graders had heard of it and were trying to make the guest list.

"Please, oh please, Zibby. Let me come to your party and I'll clean your cleats the entire year," begged a shrimpy fifth grader named Davis during second recess.

Zibby shook her head. "No way. Plan your own party." This was one group of kids she didn't have to feel one bit guilty about not inviting. No respectable sixth grader would ever have fifth graders at her party. Even if one of them did promise to be her own personal shoe shiner.

Zibby was in the middle of waving off Davis when Amber appeared at Zibby's side. "If you aren't just Little Miss Party Popular," Amber said in a not-very-nice tone of voice.

"What?" asked Zibby, caught off guard by Amber's comment.

"Oh, nothing," snapped Amber. "Now, listen, Zibby," she continued, "you may have had a problem with my last party, but you have to admit, I throw really good ones."

"Yes," said Zibby, wondering why Amber was talking about her own parties and where the conversation was headed.

"In fact, I'm something of a party expert," Amber continued. "And I feel I have to let you know that I'm a teensy bit worried about *your* party."

"Really?" asked Zibby, surprised. "I thought you were happy that I was including the boys."

"Oh, the boys." Amber shrugged. "That's cool. But what I'm wondering is, what are we going to *do* at your party. I mean, it's only a little over a week away. What activities do you have planned? What will the invitations look like? Have you figured *anything* out yet?"

Zibby felt her happy bubble begin to burst. The truth was, she *hadn't* figured out any of those things. She'd been so caught up inviting people, she hadn't gotten around to even thinking about the actual party.

"No, but I'm working on it," said Zibby. "And whatever I come up with, it will be really amazing!"

Amber moved in a step closer toward Zibby. " I hope so, Zibby. I can't wait to hear your plans and see just how great this party of yours really is going to be. And I really want to see if it can possibly ever be as good as one of mine. Good luck!" she practically spat out the words as she turned around and quickly walked away.

"What's *her* problem?" Zibby asked herself. And why was Amber comparing *her* parties to Zibby's? It seemed almost as if she was trying to turn parties into a contest. Zibby knew all about competition out on the soccer field, but she didn't know that girls could feel competitive about parties. But from the way Amber was talking, it sure seemed like Amber did.

Parties aren't competitions, Zibby thought. *Or* – and then she had a Big Revelation – *maybe they are*. Maybe throwing parties *was* Amber's sport, just like playing soccer was Zibby's. And just like Zibby didn't like to lose at soccer, Amber didn't want to lose at the party game.

Suddenly Zibby got a feeling she usually only felt on the soccer field just before she was about to clobber an opponent. Because if Amber wanted a competition, she was more than happy to give her one!

* * *

Zibby went home from school that day determined to get the invitations out that very night. She pulled a graphic of a girl whispering into another girl's ear off a free clip art web site, then copied the image into a Word document. In a festive font, she typed:

Psst! Have you heard?
Everyone's coming to Zibby's for a party on the 18th
5 - 8 pm
RSVP to Zibby at 555-8769 or tomboykid@lincoln.com
PREPARE FOR A PARTY UNLIKE ANY OTHER!

Zibby wasn't so sure about the last line, since she didn't want to promise something she couldn't deliver. On the other hand, she figured, since it was her party and no one else's, and since she was inviting so many people, boys included, by definition the party *was* unlike any other.

She printed out the invitations on nice blue paper her mom bought at the stationery store, then addressed and stamped all of them.

"I'm on a roll," she said to herself with a sense of accomplishment. "Now I just have to figure out what we're going to *do*." She felt a jab of worry but quickly shrugged it off. She was full of Great Ideas. About everything. How hard could it be to come up with one little party plan after all?

CHAPTER 9

A PARTY PICKLE

"Why me?" Zibby wailed, burying her head in her hands.

It was 10:30 on Saturday morning and she'd already wasted two hours trying to come up with the Perfect Party Plan with no success. Every idea she thought of stunk, from charades (too cheesy) to Twister (too boring) to scavenger hunts (been done a million times). She even Googled "fun party games," but they were all Total Stinkers too. Like the "Extreme Version of Truth or Dare" where the dares include sticking your hand in the toilet or eating a cube of butter. *Gross!* Or the "Crazy Egg" game where players smash hard boiled eggs on their foreheads. But the joke is that some eggs are raw. *Ha, ha*, thought Zibby, *real funny*. Then there was the "Life Saver" game, where teams pass Life Savers back and forth to each other – using only their lips. *Yeah, like that might happen!*

She needed help, and she needed it fast.

She called Sarah, but Sarah wasn't home. "Typical," she thought crankily. Lately Sarah was always going off somewhere when Zibby needed her.

Next, Zibby headed to her older brother Anthony's room across the hall.

"Hey, let me in, Anthony!" she yelled as she pounded

with both fists on the door.

Anthony opened the door, rubbing his eyes and looking as if he'd just woken up. "Do you always have to scream so loud and knock like the house is on fire – especially this early in the morning?" he asked. "How about a nice gentle tap, tap tap?" He demonstrated by lightly rapping his knuckles on the door.

"You know I have a hard time being quiet," Zibby said as she barged into his room. "And so do my fists. Besides, it's not early – it's past 10! It's getting late, actually."

Anthony sighed and sat down on his bed. "So what do you want?" he asked.

"I need you to help me come up with a good idea for my party," she said. "What should I have everyone do?"

"How many are coming again?" he asked, stretching his arms. "Twenty-four, is it?"

"Make that thirty-four," said Zibby. "I had to invite ten other people – but don't tell Mom or Dad yet, okay? I'll do it later."

"Okay, but they might freak. That's a lot of people."

"Don't remind me," said Zibby impatiently. "Just tell me how I should entertain them all."

"At the parties I go to, we just listen to music and dance," he said.

"Barf!" exclaimed Zibby. "That sounds like Amber's party. Try again."

Suddenly Anthony smiled triumphantly. "I've got it! Post a big sign on the front door saying, *Party Cancelled*. Then you can run upstairs, hide beneath the covers, watch a movie on the laptop, and hope they all go home!"

"Thanks a lot." She hit him on the shoulder and not too playfully either. "Thanks a lot for absolutely nothing."

She stomped downstairs and went to ask her mom for some suggestions, but she was too busy. "I'm on deadline, honey," her mom said, hunched over her laptop in the dining room. Her mom was a freelance writer for magazines and often had to finish up her stories on the weekends. "I was actually supposed to get this in yesterday – but we can talk about your party in a few hours when I'm done."

A few hours? thought Zibby. She wanted to figure out the party – pronto!

"That's okay," Zibby said sulkily. "I'll figure it out somehow."

She was wondering if she should hit up her dad for some ideas, even though he spent most of his time at work and wasn't exactly what you'd call a Party Expert, when the doorbell rang. She ran to answer it and was surprised to see Vanessa and Franny on the front porch. "What are you guys doing here?" she asked. They were the last two people she'd expect to drop by.

"We've got something super duper important to tell you," said Franny.

"What?" asked Zibby, unable to imagine what it could be.

"We heard your party was in trouble, so we – "

"What? Who told you that?" Zibby demanded.

"Amber," replied Franny. "After school yesterday we

heard her telling Camille that your party was going to be a dud because you didn't have anything planned to do."

"She said that?" asked Zibby, fuming inside. *That Amber!* She'd show her – somehow!

"But don't worry," said Franny. "Because we're here to solve all your problems. Maybe you didn't know it, but my mom's a party planner. And she said she'd handle your party – she's got tons of activities, games, and party favors, so you're all set."

"Really?" asked Zibby.

"Yep – and it's all for free," said Vanessa, smiling.

"That's awesome!" yelled Zibby.

"It's the least we can do for you since you're letting us come," said Franny.

Zibby couldn't believe her good luck. She'd only invited Franny and Vanessa because she felt sorry for them, and now they were the ones solving her party problem! For the first time all morning, she began to feel happy. Her party was going to be a success after all! She had a *professional* planning it.

"Thanks so much, you guys," she said, giving a big smile.

"No problem," Franny said, whipping out her Sponge Bob wristwatch and checking the time. "Woops – got to run. Vanessa's mom is taking us shopping – Vanessa found this really cool 'Barney on the Farm' lunch box she wants to get."

She needs two Barney lunch boxes? Zibby wondered, intrigued. But all she said was, "Have fun!"

She shut the door and leaned against it, then let out a very big sigh of relief. But then she had a realization. She'd gotten so caught up in Franny's Big News that she forgot to ask something really important: What *kind* of party was Franny's mom going to throw?

Zibby bolted out of the house and down to the sidewalk to learn more, but the two girls were already long gone.

CHAPTER 10

THE DISTRESSING DETAILS

The first thing Zibby did Monday at school was hunt Franny down to find out what her mother was planning for her party. She couldn't wait to hear all the details of her *professionally-planned* shindig!

She found Franny and Vanessa by the monkey bars – they were practically the only two sixth graders who still liked to play on them. Franny was hanging upside down from her knees, while Vanessa was drawing Barney outlines in the sand with a stick. When they saw Zibby approach, Franny flipped off the bars and greeted Zibby with a big smile and an excited, "HI, ZIBBY!" as if she hadn't seen Zibby in years.

"Hey," said Zibby, greeting her. "Thanks again for helping me out with my party. I'm just wondering, what kind of games and favors there are going to be."

"The best ever," said Franny. "Elmo figurines, pin the nose on the clown, Disney characters, a Barney piñata, paper airplanes – everything you could ever want."

"Huh?" said Zibby. She couldn't have heard this right.

"Like I said, the best stuff ever. Some people think that kind of stuff is only for little kids, but my mom says we'll love it all because it's 'retro cool.'"

Zibby's mouth fell open. *Elmo figurines. Pin the nose on the clown?* These things weren't 'retro cool.' They were things her three-year-old brother Sam would like, not her friends! Her party problem wasn't solved after all – it was only getting worse. She wanted to scream, "No way," but she stopped herself. She couldn't be that rude to Franny, who, after all, thought she was helping. She had to get out of Franny's party gently and kindly. And by telling a big fat lie.

"You won't believe this," Zibby said, "but I just remembered that I don't need your mom's help after all. I figured out the party all on my own this weekend, so please tell your mom thanks, but no thanks. I really won't be needing her." Zibby turned around quickly to make her escape.

"Wait a minute," yelled Franny. "What are you talking about? Even if you've got some things planned, you can still use my mom's help."

Zibby turned back around and sighed. She'd have to try another lie. "I just don't want to put your mom out," she pleaded. "She probably works so hard – "

"It's no trouble," interrupted Franny. "She wants to help you. She can't wait to help you. She's excited."

"I really can't trouble her," Zibby repeated. " So will you please give her a big thank you from me and tell her maybe she can help out at my next party or something ... maybe when she has more time?"

Franny put her hands on Zibby's shoulder and stared into her eyes. "Oh, Zibby. Will you stop being so darned considerate? I won't take no for an answer. And neither will my mom."

"And neither will I!" Vanessa leapt up off the ground and stood next to Franny.

Franny let go of Zibby's shoulders just as the warning bell rang. "We'll be in touch with more details," she said, and the two girls ran off to class.

That went well, thought Zibby, rolling her eyes. So much for the gentle, kind tactic. The only way she could stop Franny and her mother was to come up with her own idea – a real one – that was so good it would convince Franny that Zibby didn't need her mother. But of course, the problem was that she still didn't know what to do at the party!

Slowly and miserably she began walking to class when Amber passed by wearing her iPod and silently mouthing song lyrics into her hairbrush as if it was a microphone. Then Amber stopped right in front of her and burst into the chorus of "You've Got the Music in Me" from *High School Musical II*. *How annoying*, thought Zibby. *Like I really want to listen to Amber's screechy soprano. Can't she save her singing for the shower?*

But then, Zibby did a double-take and her eyes fell on the hairbrush again. Despite her initial annoyance, she began to smile. Then she smiled bigger. Because finally, and with thanks to Amber, she'd found her party idea. Now all she had to do was make sure it would work!

* * *

When Zibby got home from school that afternoon, she ran into the kitchen and pulled out the phone book. She went right to the *k*'s and looked up "Karaoke Machine Rentals," because she'd decided to have a karaoke party. Everyone liked karaoke, even the boys. Once, the teachers brought in a karaoke machine at lunch as a reward for good test scores, and it was mobbed. And so far, no one in the sixth grade had ever thrown a karaoke party. After all her party planning stress, she'd finally come up with The Absolute Best Idea!

She found several companies that rented machines, and started dialing. The first place said they were out of rentals; a cranky lady at the second store said she didn't rent to kids and then hung up. But Zibby had better luck at the third rental company – Everyone's A Star.

"I'd like to rent a karaoke machine for next Saturday," she said politely when a man answered.

"What kind?" he asked in a warm, friendly voice that sounded promising. "We've got some small ones with a few thousand songs, up to our deluxe professional model with over 20,000 songs."

"How much are they to rent?" she asked.

"That depends – the small one goes for $100 and the professional one for $350."

One hundred dollars? Her parents would barely go for that, let alone $350. She had to get the small one even though she really wanted the deluxe model. Oh well, it was still karaoke!

"I'll take the cheapest one," she said firmly.

"You got it. Name, please," the man said.

"Zibby Payne."

"How do you spell it? P-A-Y-N-E?"

"That's right," said Zibby, impressed. Usually people spelled it P-A-I-N, which really bugged her.

"Funny," said the man. "Just the other day I was meeting with my accountant, Jackson Payne, who spells his name the same way."

"That's my dad," shouted Zibby. "Well, at least that's his name and he *is* an accountant."

"Must be the same person," he said. "Your dad's been my accountant for years."

"That's nice," said Zibby, starting to feel impatient. She didn't want to get dragged down in small talk – she wanted to get on with renting the machine.

"You're his daughter and you're throwing a party?" he asked.

"Yes," she said. "And let me tell you, it's super stressful. So if you don't mind, I'd really like to get the entertainment part all set so I can quit worrying about it."

"You can quit worrying right now," said the man. "Your dad has been good to me and we've become friends, so I'd be happy to rent you the deluxe karaoke machine. For free."

"No way!" said Zibby. "Are you serious?"

"Yes. In fact, I'll call your dad right now and make all the arrangements," he said.

"That's amazing – thank you so much," said Zibby, hanging up the phone and doing a little dance around the kitchen. *Hallelujah!* She was going to have a professional karaoke machine with 20,000 songs for her party – all for free. And even better, she now had a reason to call off Franny's mom. She found Franny's name in the school directory and gave her a call. When Franny answered, Zibby launched right into her Farewell to Elmo & Barney Speech.

"Franny, guess what? I'm having a karaoke party – I just arranged it – with a professional state-of-the art karaoke machine. So really, I won't need your mom anymore. But please tell her I appreciate it anyway."

"You'll still need games and party favors," Franny said.

"No, I really don't – " Zibby started to say, but Franny cut her off.

"Like I said before, Zibby, I won't take no for an answer. And in fact, we have something else planned for your party as well. Vanessa's taking this hip-hop tap dance class, and she learned this really cool line dance called the Funky Donkey. She's agreed to teach it to everyone at your party. You don't even need tap shoes to do it! And there is this cutest little 'hee haw' you get to say in the middle. It's adorable!"

A "Funky Donkey" dance? thought Zibby in horror. She just couldn't see Amber and the other girls stomping around saying "hee haw." No way!

"Listen, Franny – "

"Don't start that whole 'being considerate' thing

again cuz I'm just not going to listen to it," interrupted Franny. "My mom is planning your party and I don't want to talk about it anymore. Now goodbye!" and she hung up.

Zibby just stood there looking at the phone in shock. Even though she really *did* have a party plan now, Franny and Vanessa were still insisting on *their* stupid party plans. They just wouldn't listen, no matter what she said. It was almost as if they were trying to wreck her party. Oh how she wished she'd *never* invited them!

CHAPTER 11

THE GUEST LIST SHRINKS

The next day at school, Zibby pretended Franny and Vanessa weren't involved in her party planning. She'd figure a way to get out of it ... somehow! But right now she just wanted to tell everyone about the professional deluxe karaoke machine with 20,000 songs. "And it's got a high-definition sound and an echo function," Zibby said. She really didn't know exactly what that meant, but it sounded good.

"Cool!" said Grace.

"You've really done it, Zibby," said Savannah. "This *will* be the party of the year!"

"Sign me up for 'You Ain't Nothing But a Hound Dog,'" said Matthew. "Elvis is the man!"

"I can't wait to sing. 'You Are The Music In Me,'" said Kelsey.

"That's *my* song," snapped Amber, folding her hands across her chest. Unlike everyone else, she didn't seem very impressed with the karaoke machine announcement. She sat down on the blacktop and organized her containers of Groovy Grapilicious lip gloss as if it was a task of national importance. But that didn't bother Zibby – she just figured Amber was jealous.

The only person Zibby told about Franny and Vanessa's unwanted offer of help was Sarah. And she made sure to do it as the two were walking home from school, so no one else would listen in and learn that Zibby's party still had a few kinks that needed to be worked out.

"So after insisting on those stupid baby toys and games," she told Sarah, "now Franny's saying Vanessa is going to do this Funky Donkey dance. It's some horrible tapping hip-hop dance where you say 'hee haw' in the middle," she fumed. Zibby expected 100 percent sympathy from Sarah, but that's not what she got.

"How do you know it's such a bad dance?" Sarah asked in a sharp voice. "Maybe it's cute."

"Cute? Are you crazy?" Zibby exploded. "A dance called the Funky Donkey has to be the dorkiest thing ever!"

Sarah pressed her lips together and looked annoyed. Zibby hadn't the faintest idea why.

They walked in silence for a minute or two. Then Zibby asked, "Want to help my mom and me plan the food?" She was hoping that the conversation might get back to normal if she switched topics. She'd gotten a Very Good Idea about the food too, now that her good ideas were flowing again.

The two girls had arrived at the corner where Sarah's house was in one direction, Zibby's in another.

"No, thanks," Sarah said rather huffily, Zibby thought. "I've got to be somewhere, but Ill help you set up for the party if you want." And then she hurried off down the street.

There she is running off again, thought Zibby, feeling irritated.

Once home, however, Zibby forgot all about Sarah because she got so wrapped up in planning the food. She'd decided that one restaurant and one restaurant alone could cater her party: The Oaks – the best place in town. But to pull it off, she needed the help of Grandma Betty, who was a regular customer at The Oaks. She'd probably spent about $10,000 over the years on her usual order of butter lettuce salad with the dressing on the side, filet mignon – served medium rare – and her signature drink, a "Spit On It" – a diet cola with a splash of lemon juice. The restaurant should be happy to pay her back by catering her beloved granddaughter's party – at a discount, of course!

But her mom was skeptical when Zibby told her the plan. "It's a bit late to be asking the restaurant for that, don't you think?" she asked. "Anyway, I was thinking of just ordering pizza."

"Everyone has pizza at their parties," protested Zibby. "Can we at least try the Oaks?"

"I guess so, but let me handle it with your grandmother," her mother said. She knew better than to argue against one of Zibby's Very Good Ideas.

"Thanks," Zibby said as her mom grabbed the phone and went out on the back porch to talk to Grandma Betty. A few minutes later, she walked inside with a big smile on her face. "Good news," she said. "Grandma Betty agreed to ask the manager, and he said yes. The restaurant is going to cater the party with steak and shrimp shish kebabs and rice for twenty-four people – for half off. I thought your plan was a total stretch, but it worked. Congratulations!"

"That's awesome!" Zibby yelled.

But the next moment, her happiness deflated like a soccer ball someone had let the air out of.

What had her mom said? The restaurant was sending shish kebabs for *twenty-four*? But there were *thirty-four* guests coming. And that's when she remembered she'd never told her parents about the extra guests. So right then and there she had to give the Big Confession to her mom. About the extra guests. And the boys. And the extra food that would be needed unless they wanted people to starve to death!

After she explained everything to her mother, something curious happened. Her mom didn't get mad. Instead, she looked concerned – about her.

"This party's been a lot of work and worry for you, hasn't it?" she asked quietly.

"YES!" yelled Zibby.

"You know, you've done enough," her mom said. "Let me take over for now. I'll figure out the extra food with The Oaks and talk to any parents who may have concerns about the boys coming over. I wish you had told me sooner about this, but I get why you did it. So now why don't you quit worrying about everything and try to relax a little before your party."

"That would be great, thanks," said Zibby. It was nice

to have someone else think about her party for once because planning it had been a lot harder than she could ever have imagined. She started to head upstairs to chill out by listening to the Eagles, when the doorbell rang.

She backtracked and opened the door. It was Franny and Vanessa – again! *What do they want?* she asked herself grumpily. But then she had a cheerful thought. "Are you here because you've changed your mind about Franny's mom?" Zibby asked.

"Not at all," said Franny. "My mom's got all the stuff ready whenever you need it – she even scored the cutest Polly Pocket stuff and found this really cool collector's item Cookie Monster game where you feed the Cookie Monster these adorable little cookies!"

"I don't think we'll be needing those – " Zibby tried to break in, but Vanessa interrupted.

"Actually we're here because we have to ask you something," Vanessa said. "My two cousins are coming for the weekend and I'm bringing them to your party. Is that okeedokey?"

And do they have blobs in their teeth and carry Barney lunch boxes too? Zibby thought sarcastically. Then her very next thought was: *We don't have enough shish kebabs for them!*

"Actually, we're a bit tight on food," she said.

"They won't eat, I swear," promised Vanessa.

Franny smacked Vanessa on the arm. "Liar! They eat like horses. Better get double portions for them, Zibby."

Great, thought Zibby. She could just see Vanessa's

cousins reaching for handfuls of shish kebabs and leaving the other guests, the ones she'd actually invited, with nothing! She had to get out of having Vanessa's cousins at her party – and out of everything else Franny and Vanessa wanted to provide, even if it meant being brutally honest.

She took a deep breath and said, "I am so sorry. I just don't think – " when Franny interrupted her.

"And Zibby," she said, "we need your help on one more little thing. We lost your invitations, and I say your party is on the 18th, but Vanessa says it's on the 25th."

"I can't believe we don't remember. Duh!" huffed Vanessa.

"It's the eigh – " Zibby started to say automatically, then she caught herself. And then, before she was fully aware of what she was doing, she blurted out, "It's the 25th."

"Told ya, so, bozo." Franny bopped Vanessa on the arm. "Thanks, Zibby, we gotta run. See you on the 25th!" And the girls took off down the street.

Zibby sat down on the front stoop and shook her head as if it had become filled with a tangled soccer net. She tried to comprehend what she'd just done. Because as unbelievable as it seemed, she, the Champion of Fair & Equal Parties, had just *un*invited two guests.

CHAPTER 12

PARTY TIME!

The next day at school, every time Zibby saw Vanessa and Franny, she meant to tell them that the party was really this Saturday the 18th and not on the 25th. But she kept finding reasons not to. Like that it was their fault for pushing their toys and dance and Gluttonous Cousins on her when she didn't want them. Or that since they really weren't her friends, she was under no obligation to invite them because it didn't go against the original spirit of her party since the party was only for friends.

It wasn't that Zibby didn't feel guilty. She did. She never meant to hurt Franny and Vanessa.

But overall, she felt relieved. Relieved that now she could have the party she wanted. Without interference. And while she knew that at some point she'd have to face Franny and Vanessa and pay the price for what she'd done, there was so much to do to get ready for the thirty-two guests, she didn't have time to dwell on her two uninvited ones.

* * *

The day of the party, Howard Symonds, owner of Everyone's A Star, came to set up the karaoke machine.

"We can't thank you enough for doing this," Zibby's father said as he shook Mr. Symonds's hand warmly.

"I'm happy to help," said Mr. Symonds.

He connected the machine to the TV and showed Zibby and her dad, who was acting as DJ for the event, how to select songs and lyrics, which then appeared on the screen. "This machine works great and is really easy to run," said Mr. Symonds. "The only thing you have to watch out for is the microphone that plugs into it. The input jack has been acting a little funny lately, so please treat the mike gently."

"Don't worry," said Zibby, reaching for the microphone and holding it carefully in her hands. "We'll be super careful."

Sarah came over early to help Zibby put out the chips and lemonade and push back the furniture so that all the guests would fit in the living room, but she was in a weird mood. She hardly said a word, and when she did, she snapped at Zibby. Zibby would have worried about it more, but her thoughts were too focused on the party. She figured that Sarah was still upset about the Funky Donkey comments, and she promised herself that someday, when the party was over, she'd finally get to the bottom of that one.

At 5:00 on the dot, the doorbell rang. Zibby ran to answer it and there stood Amber, Camille, and Kelsey, dressed identically in short skirts, platform shoes, and enough lip gloss to cause an oil spill should they by some chance fall into the ocean.

"Hi. Now let me at that karaoke machine," said Amber, pushing past Zibby and into the living room.

"It's all yours," said Zibby, stepping aside.

"Me, too," demanded Kelsey, also brushing by Zibby.

"Wait for me, guys," cried Camille, tailing behind them.

A minute or two later, another group of girls arrived, and another, and soon the living room was full of chatter. Zibby and her parents passed around drinks and chips. Last but not least, the boys arrived. When Zibby opened the door to let them in, they stood sheepishly in a bunch, looking too nervous to come inside.

"Come on in," Zibby said, grabbing Matthew by one arm and Zane by the other. "The girls won't bite."

"Well," she said, then lowered her voice and whispered just so Matthew could hear, "maybe just Amber." Matthew winked at her and continued on into the living room with the rest of the boys following.

Now that the boys were there, the party could start. Zibby made her way through the throng of girls who had surrounded the karaoke machine, then turned the mike on and addressed her guests.

"Hello, and welcome to the party," said Zibby. "I hope you're all ready to karaoke. Just pick a song and the lyrics automatically come up on the television screen. I also have a list of songs I can pass around. Now who wants to sing the first song?" She held out the mike.

"I do," cried out Amber, leaping forward. "Mr. Payne, will you please put on 'You are the Music in Me?'"

"No, *I'm* first," yelled Kelsey, following Amber on her heels. "And Mr. Payne, I'd like that song myself."

Zibby began to stumble backward as both girls rushed toward her.

"I'll take that," Amber swiped the mike from Zibby's hand.

"No you don't," grumbled Kelsey, putting her hands on the mike and tugging it toward her.

"It's mine," said Amber, wrestling the mike back.

"Mine," cried Kelsey, pulling it her way.

"Now, girls," said Mr. Payne, "please go gentle on that mike or else it might – "

But he never got to finish his sentence. Because just then, Amber put both hands back on the mike and gave it such an enormous yank that the mike came out of the plug. But not only did the cord fly off, so did the jack that attached the mike to the karaoke machine.

"Oh no – you broke it!" yelled Zibby. She ran over to the cord, lying a few feet away, and picked it up, nervously examining the dangling jack. "Now what are we doing to do?"

Amber, who was left holding the mike, dropped it down on the ground as if it was the barrel of a steaming hot curling iron. "This is all *your* fault," she said to Zibby. "You're supposed to have a sign-up sheet where people *sign up* to sing songs. If you had a sign-up sheet, this wouldn't have happened."

"Yeah, Zibby." Kelsey glared at Zibby.

The two shrugged their shoulders, straightened the

hems of their skirts and walked back to join the rest of the kids.

Mr. Payne took the cord out of Zibby's hands. "Maybe I can fix this," he said to Zibby. "What I need is ... duct tape!" and he hurried out of the room.

Zibby turned to face her guests, whose faces seemed to be set in a Collective Frown.

"Now what are we doing to do at this party?" asked Lyla.

"Yeah?" asked Grace.

"Um," Zibby stuttered, then yelled out, "Who needs a mike anyway? We can sing karaoke without one." To prove it, she chose "Hotel California" from the song selection and began singing at the top of her lungs. But she only got out a few lines when Amber stepped up and flipped off the music.

"It's no fun without a mike," she said.

Zibby quit singing.

"Yeah," a few of the other kids mumbled.

"I once went to a karaoke club where they had two mikes for duets," said Camille.

"Yeah, you should have gotten two mikes," said Kelsey sulkily. "Then we'd still have one."

Now that everyone had rejected mike-less karaoke singing, Zibby didn't know what to do or say to fix her party. Because karaoke *was* her entire party. So she said the only thing that came to her mind: "FOOD'S SERVED! The Oaks is catering – we're having steak and shrimp shish kebabs in the kitchen. Follow me."

"The Oaks? Cool!" cried out Camille, lunging toward the kitchen.

"Yummy," said Amber, while several other kids *oohed* and *aahed*.

Zibby raced into the kitchen to make sure the food was ready, but she didn't see anything except a big bowl of rice on the counter. Her mom was checking on something in the oven.

"Where are the shish kebabs?" Zibby asked frantically. "I'm going to serve them now. Right now."

"Oh," her mom said, looking at Zibby nervously.

"What?" asked Zibby.

"I didn't have time to tell you yet. The Oaks just dropped off all the food – I stuck it in the oven to keep it warm and – turns out – they had a little problem since we had to change the order to accommodate more guests."

"*Problem?* What problem?" asked Zibby as the kids began to push open the kitchen door behind her.

"The Oaks didn't have enough shish kebabs for everyone so instead, they sent us ... fish sticks."

CHAPTER 13

SOMETHING'S FISHY

"Fish sticks?" yelled Zibby. "But we ordered steak and shrimp!"

"I know," said her mom, pulling a big tin from the oven and pouring the fish sticks onto platters. "But there's nothing I can do about it."

"We've been cheated!" said Zibby.

"Don't worry," her mom said. "They're *gourmet* fish sticks – that's what the manager said. Plus, people don't really care about what they eat at parties. They just want to be with their friends and have fun."

"I hope you're right," said Zibby as she quickly put a platter out on the table just as the guests, led by Camille, burst through the door.

Camille took one look at the food and announced, "These aren't shish kebabs. These are fish sticks!"

"*Gourmet* ones," Zibby quickly said. "We had a tiny problem with the caterers, but these are great. You'll love them."

Camille frowned. "I'll just eat some rice," she said grumpily.

"Yuck," said Kelsey, who was next in line. She picked up a fish stick gingerly with her thumb and index finger.

"They look like the frozen ones my mom gets when she doesn't want to cook." She dropped the piece back down on the plate.

"Where's my surf and turf?" asked Lyla as the kids all crowded together to get a better look at the food.

"Did you know that the batter on one fish stick contains all the grease and fat you're supposed to eat in an entire week?" Amber declared in a loud voice. "Basically it's like eating a tub of fried butter."

"Gross!" said a few of the girls in unison.

So much for her mom saying guests don't care about the food, thought Zibby morosely. *Everyone was acting as if she was trying to poison them!* She was just about to take away the platters and dump them in the sink when Matthew reached over and piled a few fish sticks on his plate. "Get out of the way, you wimps," he said. "I'll eat them."

"Thank you," Zibby mouthed to Matthew, hoping that some of the other kids would quit being so picky.

She couldn't bear to watch the Fish Stick Fiasco anymore, so she went back into the living room to check on her dad. She found him sitting cross-legged on the floor, trying to tape the cord back into the jack. When he saw her, he sighed. "I'm sorry, Zibs," he said. "I don't think it's going to work. I can tape the jack back into the machine, but the connection is broken and the mike still doesn't work."

Just great, she thought, but to her dad, she said, "Thanks for trying." After all, it wasn't his fault Amber and Kelsey had a grabbing fit over the mike. Then she flung herself down into a chair that had been pushed to the side of the room to make way for the karaoke singers. After a few minutes, Sarah appeared from the kitchen and sat down in a chair next to her. "That really stinks about the mike and the shish kebabs," Sarah said. But she didn't sound all that sad about it.

"Yeah," said Zibby, too upset to say anything else.

"By the way, what happened to Vanessa and Franny?" asked Sarah, shooting her a funny look. "I don't see them anywhere."

"Oh, I don't know," Zibby fibbed, not wanting to talk about them right now at all.

"Isn't it strange that they aren't here?" Sarah persisted.

"I don't know and I don't care!" yelled Zibby. They were the last two people she wanted to think about right now, or ever!

CHAPTER 14

PARTY CRASHERS

Zibby slumped down in her chair. The mere mention of Franny and Vanessa made her feel horribly guilty, and right now, she just couldn't handle feeling bad about one more thing. If she didn't do something soon, her party would go down as the worst in the history of Lincoln Elementary – but she was fresh out of ideas about how to fix it.

Suddenly the doorbell rang, which snapped Zibby out of her funk. *Who could* that *be?* she asked herself grumpily. Everyone she'd invited was already there.

She sighed and dragged herself across the living room toward the door when a familiar face popped up in the entry hall window. Then a second one. And this one was wearing three pigtails. *Franny and Vanessa!* They were outside her house right now!

"What are *they* doing here?" she asked herself. Either they came to catch her in a lie, or they'd gotten mixed up and shown up on the correct night despite what she'd told them. Either way, the situation was capital *A*-awkward. So Zibby decided to do the only thing she could think of: act as if nothing was wrong.

She raced across the entry hall and flung the door

open. Franny and Vanessa jumped a bit, caught off guard by the sudden opening of the door. Behind them on the front lawn, two boys were dribbling a soccer ball back and forth.

"Come on in," Zibby said extra cheerfully. "Everyone's inside." At least, Zibby noticed, they weren't carrying any toys, and Vanessa didn't have on tap shoes, but she was carrying a shopping bag. Maybe they'd figured it out on their own how bad their party ideas were. This could be Zibby's first break of the evening – and did she ever need it!

But her hopes that anything good was going to happen that night rapidly vanished when she noticed the frowns on Franny and Vanessa's faces. Gigantic ones. Like they'd never be able to smile again, even if the government outlawed school and declared a State of Constant Summer.

"What are you waiting for?" Zibby asked, her voice a little less bright.

"We know what you did," Franny said angrily.

"Yeah, we're not idiots!" said Vanessa.

Zibby quickly closed the front door behind her and stepped out onto the front porch. "I'm really sorry," she started to say, but Franny interrupted her. "Did you really think we wouldn't find out the party is *tonight*?" she asked. "Especially since Sarah told us the correct date?"

How did Sarah get involved? Zibby wondered. But she didn't have time to ponder that question because Franny just kept on going. "How do you think we felt when we realized you told us the wrong date on purpose?" asked Franny. "I guess you're just like everyone else and decided you didn't want us 'losers' at your party!"

"No," protested Zibby. "That's not it at all!"

"Yeah, right," snorted Franny. "And just for the record, my parents, grandparents, aunts, uncles, cousins, and my great-aunt Olivia, too, all hate you again!"

"What about Kendall, your great-aunt's nephew once-removed who lives out of state?" Zibby asked in a small voice.

"Yeah, him too!" Franny yelled.

"And my cousins hate you too," said Vanessa. "And they're definitely not going to teach you how to do the super secret soccer moves that they learned in all-star camp last summer."

Zibby blew air out of her cheeks and sat down on the front steps. She looked up at Franny and Vanessa, who, silhouetted against the darkness by the porch light, each looked about ten feet tall.

"I don't blame you for being mad at me," said Zibby, "But I can explain, really ..." Then she hesitated, because if she told them the truth about why she disinvited them, that would hurt their feelings too. She'd gotten herself into an Impossible Mess – a mess she didn't even have time for right now, considering that what she really needed to be doing was getting back inside and trying to salvage her pitiful party. But before she could figure out what to say, Franny started talking again.

"We're not going to let you get away with it, Zibby.

So we came anyway, with all our party stuff, even though you don't deserve it. Because when we make promises, we stick to them."

Franny marched over to the sidewalk and picked up an oversized Talbot's bag and Barney piñata that Zibby hadn't noticed before, then came back and stood in front of her. Franny set the piñata on the ground, then pulled out a small Elmo figurine and thrust it in Zibby's face.

"See?" Franny asked, then put the Elmo back inside the bag.

"Yeah, see?" repeated Vanessa, leaning down and pulling a pair of tap shoes and something shiny and blue from her bag. "You don't deserve the Funky Donkey dance either, it's so good. But I'm gonna do it because I don't back out of commitments like *some other people* we know!"

Zibby couldn't believe that now, after everything she'd done to avoid Franny and Vanessa's party plans, at the last minute, she was still getting stuck with the baby toys and the donkey dance. No way! Not after the night she'd had. "NO!" she yelled. "No Elmos and no Funky Donkey dance! That's why I disinvited you."

"What?" asked Franny.

"At least you know it's not because I think you're losers," said Zibby. "Because I don't. It was because I didn't want your mom to plan my party!"

Franny stared at her blankly, as if Zibby had just spoken another language. "You don't like Elmo?" Franny asked. "Everyone likes Elmo. He's retro cool. I told you!"

"I don't think he's cool," yelled Zibby. "Or that stupid donkey dance either!"

Vanessa opened her mouth, then closed it, and a tear rolled down her cheek. Then she threw her shoes and dress in the shopping bag and ran down the sidewalk.

"Now look what you've done, Zibby," said Franny. "You're worse than Amber or Savannah or any of those snots. Way worse!" She threw her sack of toys down on the ground, turned around, and ran off after Vanessa. The cousins looked up from their soccer dribbling in surprise, then followed Franny.

"I am not," Zibby yelled. "No way!"

But as she stood alone on the porch, looking at the Talbot's bag, from which Elmo had spilled out and seemed to be staring at her – and judging her with its black pupil-less eyes – she was forced to reconsider.

CHAPTER 15

ELMO RULES

Zibby sat down on the porch and thought about what Franny had said.

Worse than Amber and Savannah and their snotty parties? Her?

Could it be true?

Well, she hadn't given away special coupons to special guests at her party, but she *had* disinvited people. Amber and Savannah had never done that. And maybe she hadn't had a "secret" part to her party, but she *had* driven away guests in tears. Amber and Savannah had never done that either.

So maybe she *was* worse.

No, not maybe. She had to be honest with herself – for sure. For double sure.

And then she realized what she had to do. It probably meant even more disaster for her party, but she didn't care. Because even though her party appeared to be past saving, maybe – just maybe – it wasn't too late to save her idea of Fair & Equal Parties. She raced out down the sidewalk in search of Franny and Vanessa.

"Wait a minute," she called out, running as fast as she could. .

She caught up with them as they were regrouping at the corner.

"Stop, will you? Please stop!" Zibby pleaded.

"What - do - you - want - now?" asked Franny, turning around, out of breath.

"To tell you to forget what I just said!" Zibby panted. "I didn't know what I was talking about, and I take it all back. My party needs help and I think your toys and party favors can save it. So please, come back."

"But you just said how uncool they were!" said Franny.

"I was wrong," said Zibby. "Really wrong. And Vanessa, please forget what I said about the Funky Donkey. I didn't tell you this, but my karaoke machine broke and there is no entertainment and my party is totally falling apart and I really need you to start some dancing."

"You said the dance was stupid," sniffed Vanessa.

"I know," said Zibby. "But can you just please pretend I didn't say it. Please, I've rethought everything and I take it all back." She looked at Vanessa hopefully, who looked at Franny, who looked at Zibby.

Then one of the cousins spoke up. "Anything to eat at this party?" he asked.

"Yes," Zibby said quickly. "Gourmet fish sticks – the best in town."

"Dude, I love fish sticks," he said to the other boy. "Let's go," he said, walking back toward Zibby's house.

Franny and Vanessa were still holding back.

"What do you think, Vanessa?" Franny asked.

"Okeedokey, I guess," she said.

"All right!" yelled Zibby. She grabbed both girls by the arm and began to gently pull them after the cousins. But when they got to the front porch, there was nothing there. The toys and the piñata were missing!

"Where'd everything go?" cried Franny.

Zibby noticed the front door was cracked open. "Maybe someone took the stuff inside," she said, giving the door a shove and stepping into the house.

As she did, she almost tripped over Amber, Camille, Savannah, and Kelsey, who were sitting in the entry hall sifting through the toys and games. The floor was littered with Elmo figurines, stuffed Grovers, the pin the nose on the clown game, the Cookie Monster Game complete with teensy cookies, Transformers, Strawberry Shortcake stickers, a Polly Pocket playhouse and car, plastic Dumbos, and a miniature set of Snow White and the Seven Dwarfs.

Amber looked up at Zibby. Zibby prepared herself for one of Amber's cutting comments, but instead Amber gushed," I luv, luv, luv these. Elmo is *so* my favorite. Grover too. Where did you get them?"

"Um," Zibby couldn't talk for a second, she was so startled by Amber's reaction. Then she began to smile. "They came from Franny!" she said. "Aren't they great? Her mom's a professional party planner and she brought all these totally retro cool toys." She turned to look at Franny. Franny actually smiled back!

"And have you seen the Cookie Monster game?" Zibby continued. "It's a genuine collector's item."

"The Cookie Monster rocks!" yelled Camille. "I watched him every morning before pre-school. Who wants to play with me?"

"I do," cried Kelsey. "And then, let's play some Polly Pockets," she picked up a car. "Look – a Totally Trendy Pets Wild Ride Safari Car!"

"You know, Zibby," Amber said with a smirk, "your party might almost end up being as good as one of mine."

"Thanks," said Zibby, smiling. For Amber, that was a pretty huge admission.

Meanwhile Katherine had discovered the piñata, which was leaning against the entryway table. "What's in it?" she asked Franny, giving it a shake.

"My mom's special mix called 'Chocolate Lovers Delight,'" said Franny. "Butterfinger balls, Nestle Crunch bars, and white chocolate M&Ms."

"I'm in chocolate heaven!" squealed Katherine. "When can we break it open?"

"Anytime you want," said Franny. And the two went out in back to find a tree from which to string up Barney.

"What's going on in here?" Matthew popped into the entry hall with Zane and another boy named Drew. When he saw Vanessa's cousins with their soccer ball, he yelled out, "Who wants to play soccer?"

"I do," Zane and Drew both said.

"Let's get a game on then," said one of the cousins. "Just as soon as I get something to eat."

"Food's in the kitchen," said Zibby, pointing him in the right direction.

Matthew and the rest of the boys began to make their way out to the front lawn. "Smart move, bringing in the soccer players, tomboy," Matthew said as he walked past her.

"I know," she said happily. Finally her guests were having fun – compliments of Franny and Vanessa, no less! Even the fish sticks were going over better.

"Sorry for my bad manners earlier," Lyla apologized as she ran by nibbling on one. "Forget surf and turf, I'm a Shake 'N Bake girl now!"

Zibby smiled. *I just might pull off a great party after all*, she said to herself.

But then she saw something that made her doubtful. Vanessa was emerging from the bathroom wearing a tight blue dress with sequins, tap shoes, and ... a donkey tail!

CHAPTER 16

GRAPEVINE TO THE LEFT

"I didn't realize a tail was part of your act," Zibby said, rushing up to Vanessa and hoping she was doing a good job of covering up her shock.

"I brought it just for tonight," said Vanessa.

Zibby wanted to say so many things, but instead she managed a stifled, "Great."

Vanessa quickly walked over to the karaoke machine and put in her CD. Click, click, click went her heels. Swish, swish, swish went her tail.

"I'm ready to dance," said Vanessa. "Should we tell everyone to come over here?"

"Sure," said Zibby in what she hoped was an enthusiastic tone. Her party was finally on a roll and she'd rather wear a Cinderella ball gown than let Vanessa funky donkey, but at this point, there was nothing she wouldn't do to make Vanessa happy and undo all the damage she'd done.

Zibby walked into the entry hall and then to the backyard to announce that Vanessa Heartgable was giving a special appearance and that everyone needed to come into the living room. Zibby went back inside, turned the music on, and gave Vanessa the floor. Then she nervously went to the far side of the room to watch.

"Hi, everyone," Vanessa's voice boomed across the room even without a mike. "This dance is real easy, and you don't need tap shoes even though I'm wearing them. It's called the Funky Donkey, and here's how it goes.

"On the count of one, two, three, take two steps to the left, stomp your feet together, two steps to the right, stomp your feet together," Vanessa called out. "Grapevine left. Say hee-haw. Grapevine right. Say hee-haw again. Tap your right toe at your left heel. Tap your left toe at your right heel. Turn around and wiggle your rear to the count of one, two, three, four, turn around, say 'funky donkey' as you pump your fist in the air, and then start all over again."

Zibby looked around the room to see how everyone was reacting. Personally, she thought the dance was a lot better than it had sounded, but then again, she knew nothing about dancing. So she was pleasantly surprised to see kids nodding their heads to the beat of the music and a few of them even practicing the steps on their own.

"I'll do it one more time – come join me up here whenever you're ready," Vanessa instructed before she repeated the moves.

Zibby looked around the room again, expecting at least a few people to come on up, but no one stepped forward. *Oh no, now what?* She'd dance with Vanessa herself, but everyone knows that tomboys don't dance – well, at least *this* tomboy! And not *this* dance!

She was about to plunge into Party Despair again

when Matthew slowly walked up to Vanessa, planted himself next to her, and began to dance. A few seconds later, Amber joined him.

"This is fun," Amber called out as she grapevined to the left. "Come on, get up here, my peeps!"

Camille, Kelsey, Savannah, and several other girls rushed up to join her. After a few minutes, so did Grace, Lyla, and Katherine. And before Zibby knew it, the dance floor was full. "Victory," she said to herself, clasping her hands together in relief. She was finally starting to relax when Sarah slid up next to her and asked, "So what do you think of the dance now?"

"Sarah!" cried Zibby. "Where've you been?"

"Out in back with the piñata," she said. "So now what do you think of the Funky Donkey?" she repeated.

"Not bad," said Zibby. "I admit, I was wrong. But it did sound dumb."

"It did, huh?" asked Sarah sharply.

Zibby still didn't see why Sarah was still being so sensitive about the Funky Donkey. But she did at least know why Sarah had been acting so strange all night.

"I know it was wrong to disinvite Franny and Vanessa," Zibby blurted out. "I feel terrible! But how did you find out? And when did you talk to Vanessa about it?"

But Sarah didn't answer. She began tapping her toes to the music and then made her way up to the dance floor. When she got there, she spun around, raised her eyebrows at Zibby, and began to dance.

And that's when Zibby began to clue in to why Sarah was so touchy about the Funky Donkey. And why she defended it from the very start. And how she might have gotten the opportunity to spend time with Franny and Vanessa, or at least Vanessa. Because from the way Sarah was dancing, it was clear that she had done the Funky Donkey before – many times!

CHAPTER 17

GET FUNKY WITH ME

"**W**here did you learn *that*?" Zibby asked as Sarah came off the dance floor, her face shiny with sweat after spending the last 10 minutes impressing the crowd with her expert moves.

"I've been going to the same dance class as Vanessa," she said.

"Get real!" gasped Zibby.

"All those times I was busy, I was going to my hip-hop tap dancing class."

"But why didn't you tell me?" asked Zibby.

"At first, there just wasn't the chance. Plus, I didn't know how you'd feel about it since I didn't think you'd go for the tap dancing part," said Sarah. "Then after you were so mean about Vanessa's dancing, there was no way I was going to tell you."

"I'm really sorry," said Zibby. There sure had been a lot of things to apologize for that night. This whole party had been one mistake after another ... and tons of stress. Right then and there, she vowed to never throw another party in her entire life.

"And at dance class," Sarah continued, "I learned that you told Vanessa the party was next weekend, so

I had to tell her the truth. I still can't believe you did that, Zibby!"

"I know, I really messed up," said Zibby. "But I swear, I'll never exclude anyone from anything again!"

"I hope not," said Sarah.

"I really did want the party to be for everybody ... " Zibby's voice trailed off.

"It was. For everyone but Franny and Vanessa, that is," said Sarah.

"I know," winced Zibby. "But I'm really trying to make it up to Franny and Vanessa, and I think it's working." She looked out at the dance floor where Vanessa was exuberantly whipping around her tail and Franny was rocking out holding a pair of Elmo figurines.

"That's true," said Sarah.

"And it's not like I haven't been punished for what I did – what, with the broken mike and those fish sticks," Zibby continued.

"True again," said Sarah. And for the first time that evening, she smiled.

And for the first time since Zibby had disinvited Franny and Vanessa to her party, she began to feel like herself – like the type of girl who really wouldn't leave anyone out – and she smiled back at Sarah.

"But you know, Zibby," Sarah continued. "I think you've got a little more making up to do with Franny and Vanessa, and I've come up with the perfect plan."

"You have?" asked Zibby, suddenly feeling nervous.

"First, you must agree to polish Vanessa's Barney lunch box every day at school for the rest of the month."

"What?" yelled Zibby.

"You will divide your time between playing soccer with the boys, hanging out with me, of course, and polishing Vanessa's lunch box while Vanessa and Franny swing on the monkey bars."

What's the justice in that? Zibby thought. But then, she reconsidered her recent actions. "Okay," she said. "Agreed."

"And second, you have to get out there and ... dance the Funky Donkey with me!" She grabbed Zibby's arm and began to pull her toward the dance floor.

"No way!" screamed Zibby, trying to twist out of Sarah's grasp.

"Yes way," said Sarah, keeping an iron lock on her and dragging her forward.

Lyla and Grace saw what was going on and began to call, "Go Zibby, Go Zibby!" Soon everyone in the room was chanting her name. "ZIBBY. ZIBBY. ZIBBY."

Zibby stopped struggling.

She looked around at her guests.

What could she do?

There was only one thing, she reluctantly realized, that would finally make the party 100 percent right.

She took two steps to the left, then stomped her feet together. Then she took two steps to the right, stomped her feet, and grapevined left.

"Awesome party!" Camille waved to her as she

funky donkeyed across the room. "You should throw another one next weekend too!"

"Party at Zibby's next Saturday!" cried Lyla.

"Cool!" everyone shouted.

Everyone except Zibby, that is.

Hee Haw!

THE END

Looking for more Zibby?
Check out the rest of the series:

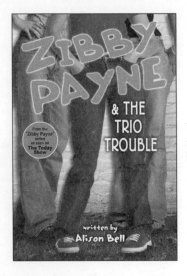

Zibby Payne
& the Trio Trouble
ISBN: 978-1-897073-78-0

When Zibby's best friend Sarah and new friend Gertrude can't get along, it becomes a Total Friendship Fiasco!

Zibby Payne
& the Drama Trauma
ISBN: 978-1-897073-47-6

Watch out Broadway, Total Tomboy Zibby has landed the lead in the sixth-grade musical. But if she doesn't stick to the script, it could be curtains for her acting career!

"... readers won't be able to put it down and parents everywhere will approve."
– *Mom Central Book Reviews*

"Zibby Payne's adventures have the humour and momentum to become a well-loved series." – *Montreal Review of Books*

Zibby Payne
& the Wonderful,
Terrible Tomboy
Experiment
ISBN: 978-1-897073-39-1

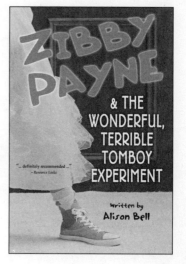

While the girls in her class obsess over lip gloss and boy bands, Zibby goes to extremes to express her True Tomboy self.

"... an outstanding character who sticks to her guns ... readers will learn ... you don't have to change for others to like you, and you should be proud of who you are."
– Bildungsroman Book Blog

"Bell has created a girl who's not afraid to be herself. A rare treat."
– Mary Hogan, author of **The Serious Kiss**

About the author: Alison Bell got her start as an editor at *'TEEN* magazine. She's written for *YM*, *Sassy*, and the *Los Angeles Times*, and is also the author of **Let's Party!** and **Fearless Fashion** from the "What's Your Style?" series (see the next page for info!). Alison lives just outside of Los Angeles in South Pasadena, California.

Visit her online at alisonbellauthor.com

Also from Alison Bell – the "What's Your Style?" Series

Let's Party
ISBN: 978-1-894222-99-0

Need ideas for your next big bash? **Let's Party!** provides eight cool and complete party plans, like the "Sensational Spa" and the "Spy Thriller Party." With mix n' match party concepts, quizzes, and troubleshooting tips, this is the essential guide for every hostess with the mostest.

"Suggestions are included for food (with recipes), small favors, and 'the setting,' but the emphasis is on the activities ... preparing for the party looks at least as fun as the event itself ..." – *The InGram*

"The ideas are fresh and simple enough for the hostess to accomplish on her own ... This manual is sure to fly off shelves." – *School Library Journal*

Fearless Fashion
ISBN: 978-1-894222-86-0

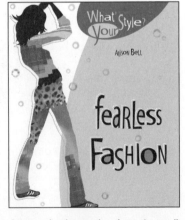

Ever wonder where different styles come from, and which one suits you best? While deconstructing today's hottest looks, **Fearless Fashion** gives you tidbits of fashion history, shows you trendy celebs and the styles they embrace, and offers creative ways to personalize any look. Includes fun quizzes to take with your friends!

"Girls will enjoy thumbing through this book as their first step into the world of fashion." – *School Library Journal*

"... ideas to adapt looks from 'preppy' to 'punk,' to make them uniquely one's own." – *Publishers Weekly*